COMMUNION

STEVE STRED

BVP

PRAISE FOR STEVE STRED

Dark, gritty coming of age that grabs you near the end and doesn't let you go.'

Justin M. Woodward, Author of Tamer Animals about *The Girl Who Hid in the Trees*

'Brutal! Dark! Cults! Short! Novella! Twisted! Messed Up! Weird! Devils! Biblical! Ceremonies!'

Char from Char's Horror Corner about *Ritual*

'Ritual is a twisted, brutal novella that combines elements of extreme and subtle horror in a perfect blend.'

Jeremy Hepler, Bram Stoker Nominated Author of The Boulevard Monster about *Ritual*

'If you weren't scared of the woods after reading Steve Stred's excellent The Girl Who Hid in the Trees, then there's no doubt you will be after reading The Stranger.'

Morgan K. Tanner, Author of Army of Skin about *The Stranger*

'Wagon Buddy has a great ending and some awesome imagery. Though it's a simple story, it's a memorable one.'

J.H. Moncrieff, Author of Those Who Came Before about *Wagon Buddy*

'Yuri has the flavour of a dark, forgotten fairy tale from the frozen heart of Russia, and the writing is every bit as compelling as I've come to expect from Stred's stories.'

Christopher Henderson, Author of Artemis One-Zero-Five about *YURI*

'A grim, frost-bitten read, with a sense of icy hope at the core of its black, withered heart.'

David Sodergren, Author of The Forgotten Island about *Piece of Me*

'The One That Knows No Fear is a story that was literally dripping with nostalgia and horror in equal measure.'

Ross Jeffery, Author of Juniper about *The One That Knows No Fear*

'Ritual is a fast and thrilling dive into the depraved mind of a man and his dogma. It draws you into the horrors of a mysterious cult, and doesn't let go until the very last page. I loved this story.'

Sonora Taylor, Author of *Without Condition* and *Little Paranoias: Stories*

Copyright © 2020 by Steve Stred All rights reserved.

No part of this book may be reproduced in any form or by any electronic or mechanical means, including information storage and retrieval systems, without written permission from the author, except for the use of brief quotations in a book review. This is a work of fiction. Names, characters, places, and incidents are a product of the author's imagination. Locales and public names are sometimes used for atmospheric purposes. Any resemblance to actual people, living or dead, or to businesses, companies, events, institutions, or locales is completely coincidental.

ISBN: 978-1-7771571-1-1

Cover art by Mason McDonald

Copy editing by David Sodergren

Formatted by Ross Jeffery

1st Edition

Black Void Publishing

For DIE!mond.
Thank you for your support!

Job 1:7
The Lord said to Satan, "Where have you come from?"
Satan answered the Lord, "From roaming throughout the
earth, going back and forth on it."

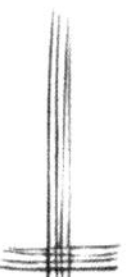

Detective Marvin McKay sat at his desk looking at the shit show of reports and photos splayed out in disarray.

It had been a week since the discovery of the aftermath at the commune. Four other groups had committed mass suicides at the same time, but those turned out to be unrelated. For that he was thankful. It meant he wouldn't have to meet with other detectives, wouldn't have to read through hundreds of group emails every day.

But Jesus fucking Christ was he struggling with what he'd seen.

His partner, Kramer, had up and drove home from the scene of the crime, wrapped a length of rope around his neck, and stepped off the landing of his two-story house. A year from retirement, and he chose to leave without even a cake.

"What the fuck!" He yelled out, startling the officers who were still mulling around the precinct at three in the morning.

Wiping the spit from his lips, McKay shook his head and decided now was as good a time as any to refill his coffee.

Leaving his office, he saw a few eyes dart his way, but the officers knew to keep their distance.

Had he slept since learning Kramer hung himself? He didn't think so. He didn't care, he just wanted to figure out what the fuck had happened, and how to prevent this from turning into a full-blown copy-cat situation.

Reports from around the country had trickled across their desks. In Florida, a group of twenty-five males had chanted the name 'Sheol' over and over before opening fire on a church. Police had arrived and through returned gunfire, killed all of the men. The only thing that McKay found intriguing was that the men were nude from the neck down, their penises cut off, and they'd been wearing wooden masks. Similar to what they found near the altar in the basement of that pseudo temple.

McKay believed it was copycat bullshit. Unfortunately, video from the complex had already hit the internet.

Grabbing a cheap, shitty Styrofoam cup, he grabbed the carafe and poured some lukewarm coffee in, then followed that with four tablespoons of sugar, just enough to make it not taste like sewage.

As he walked back to his office, McKay caught the shape of someone standing near the intake desk. Stopping, he leaned back to get a better view.

Admiring the ass displayed in the tight dress, he changed course and made his way to the front desk.

"Officer Douglas, you need a hand here with this lady?" McKay asked, trying to sound chipper.

"Thanks, McKay. She says she has some info about," Douglas looked at his notepad, "someone named Brad? Said it has to do with the Kool-Aid cult." McKay tapped his shoulder, not wanting him to use that name in front of the public.

They hadn't found any writings or documents containing anything to officially name them or label them. The media had given them a few different monikers, but for now, McKay was fine to just refer to them as a file number.

"Well, I'm the detective in charge. Let's find an open interrogation room and we can sit and talk. Unless you'd prefer my office?"

"The interrogation room would be just fine," she replied.

McKay couldn't stop staring into her eyes. He'd never seen a color so radiant. Almost yellow. He presumed contacts, everyone was wearing some sort of jewelry now.

"Just wait here. I'll go get my notepad. Douglas, grab her a coffee or something while she waits, yeah?"

McKay shuffled off, smiling at his luck. Sometimes people were so desperate, worried they'd say something and end up in jail, they'd do just about *anything* to stay out of prison.

Anything.

Entering his office, McKay slipped off his belt and hung it over his chair.

Walking back to find the woman, he was counting on her being up for whatever, tonight.

Lord knew, he needed some relief.

"Miss... I'm sorry, I didn't catch your name," McKay said, looking at the notepad Douglas had handed him.

Taking a seat across from McKay, she looked even more radiant surrounded by the darkened background.

"I didn't give it. I want to make sure I'll be protected," she replied.

"Absolutely. That's what we do."

"You didn't protect Brad. Or the other followers. Has there been any sign of Father?"

McKay stared at her for some time, rolling around his head all the connections he'd made through background checks and interviews over the week. It felt like years since Kramer discovered the aftermath already.

"Look, it's a situation that's evolving, and I'm dealing with many working parts. So, let's just cut to the chase. What do you know? How are you connected? I don't need a name if you are worried about your safety."

She gave a nod, took a sip of her coffee, then examined the room.

"It's just us here. Three am. No cameras. I'm not recording this."

That seemed to soften her, her shoulders relaxing a bit.

"My name is unimportant. I knew Brad because he was the Chosen One. I knew Father, as he was *my* father. Detective McKay, I was a member of that cult. For my entire life, I lived and breathed our mantra of opening the black heavens. Of ascendency and immortality amongst the cosmos. Of living both *here* and *there*."

McKay watched her face, not seeing any ticks or quirks. If she was lying she was doing a damn fine job of it.

"That's great and all, but why come to me? Why now?"

Now it was her turn to run some scenarios through her mind. This made McKay uneasy. He was the one who was supposed to be in control. In this room, right now, he didn't feel like he was leading.

"I know you don't believe what I've said. I can assure you, I'm telling the truth. You don't understand everything you're dealing with. You don't understand what's to come here."

She sounded like she was on the brink of a panic attack. She had suddenly grown agitated, and McKay could swear she was starting to sweat.

"OK. Let's take a breather. Are you alright? Do you need something to eat? Refill on the coffee?"

She shook her head, her breathing settling dramatically.

McKay wished she was still amped up, he enjoyed watching her ample chest push up and down, straining against that thin material.

God, what I'd do to this slut, he thought.

He didn't have time to finish his thought, as a nail

slammed through the back of his palm, easily slicing through and penetrating the table below. He screamed in agony, looking at the woman before him.

Her eyes were wide, her teeth bared.

"I'm not going to fuck you, you piece of shit," she roared as she reared back and punched him square in the nose. His face burst open, blood and cartilage flying.

"Your blood plays a role that *he* needs played," she said, as she pushed the nail further into the table.

"Help!" He yelled, trying to pry his hand free from the table, the rusted nail holding firm.

"Preacher's Rock holds the secret. Go there. Study what I've left in your office. Just know, it's watching how this unfolds. Soon it'll unfold before you."

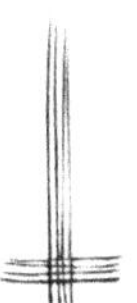

"What took so fucking long?"

McKay was furious at the slow response.

Between his hand and his nose, a lot of blood had collected on his lap and the table in the interrogation room.

The mysterious lady had disappeared and left him yelling for help for what felt like hours, his voice becoming hoarse and his throat feeling like sandpaper.

Officer Douglas had casually walked in, drinking some coffee. When he saw the extent of McKay's situation, he immediately called for a medic and then peppered McKay with questions.

Once the medic had bandaged the hand - Douglas informed McKay that the woman had vanished, but that she had in fact left a package on his desk.

"It's wrapped in butcher's paper," he'd said, nonchalantly.

"Is it fucking leaking anything?"

"Not sure."

"Not. Sure? What the actually fuck, Douglas? That bitch just broke my nose and used a four-inch nail to fuse me to the fucking table. She left something in butcher's paper and you what? Didn't even investigate it? Fuck me, expect a reduction in duties real quick. Better call your union rep, motherfucker. When I get back from the ER, I'm filing papers."

Douglas stood stunned as McKay was led to the waiting ambulance by the medic.

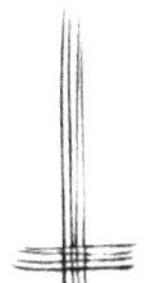

Four hours later, McKay returned to the precinct, elated to not walk in and see Douglas sitting at the intake desk.

He ignored the stares as he made his way to his office, dismayed to see that Douglas had been right – there on his desk was a wrapped package.

The brown butcher's paper sat like a square of radioactive material.

"You gonna open it?"

The voice from behind scared the shit of him, causing him to jump.

"Sorry, boss. Didn't mean to sneak up on you."

McKay looked, seeing Erickson standing there.

"All good, Erickson. I assume that loudmouth Douglas filled you in about last night's festivities?"

A quick nod answered.

McKay went and sat at his desk, staring at the package. He looked at the wrapping, the string around it and at the shape.

"You want me to call forensics? Get it dusted for prints?"

"Nah, I suspect it'll be a waste of time. I mean, fuck. How many prints did we get at that compound? Not one of them were in the system. This chick ain't going to be either."

"You sure boss? Freddie watched the tape from when she entered and he's pretty sure he hauled her in for assault a few months back."

This piqued his interest.

"Give Freddie a call, tell him we need to talk."

Erickson left, leaving the man alone with his delivery.

"Just what the fuck is in here?"

Finally, McKay worked up the nerve and grabbed one end of the bow. Pulling the string, it un-looped and fell away. Some of the brown paper popped up a bit, but McKay would have to pull it back to open it all the way.

Looking out into the work area, he could see a few officers at their desks leaning and lurching, trying to get a view.

"Whoever's interested in seeing what's in this, get over here!" He hollered out.

A bustle of activity from beyond the closed blinds of his office window led him to get up and turn the thin plastic twister to open them. The entire police force was standing on the other side.

This made him feel more confident, if not a bit worried that if a bomb was inside, the entire contingent of Precinct 32 would be eradicated with one detonation.

"Show time," he said, pulling the four corners of the paper back.

What the paper had been concealing was a very old looking box.

The gathered officers collectively leaned forward, craning to see what was on the box.

McKay looked at the lid, seeing carvings and lettering.

"What's it say?" someone called out.

McKay looked at the faces gathered around, feeling as though the room had suddenly increased in temperature.

"There's lettering carved into the top. Appears to be a stone box. It says *Nam hoc novum mundum venisti*. Is that Latin? Someone get me a translation," he asked, snapping his fingers.

"Yeah, Latin. Google Translate is showing that it means *'For a new world would come.'*"

McKay felt like his stomach contents were fighting to leave his body.

"What's carved on there?"

McKay looked at the officer who asked, wishing he'd not invited everyone to gather around.

"There is some sort of creature here. Long horns, goat-like face. The feet are hooves. Looks like the body is human," he said to the room.

"Satan?"

The noise of people murmuring agreement arose.

"I don't believe so," McKay replied. "If this has to do with what happened at the compound, nothing that we've found has been related to Satan. Even the coincidental pentagram layout from the five groups hasn't been linked to Satan."

McKay studied the carvings on the sides. They were all similar; humans kneeling, worshipping the creature on the top. He noticed the layout of the carving was such that the creature was sitting on something. A throne? Or a rock?

Preacher's Rock holds the secret. The last thing that woman had said to him was about this Preacher's Rock. McKay reached a hand out and tapped the box. It wasn't wood. It was solid stone. This stone had been carved and etched. The lettering was pristine.

"Let's open this up."

5

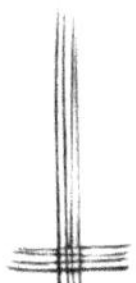

Outside, the weather changed rapidly.

While it had started out a sunny, clear day, now the clouds rolled in.

Thunder rumbled, and lightning flashed across the sky.

The rain began to fall, picking up intensity as McKay examined the stone box.

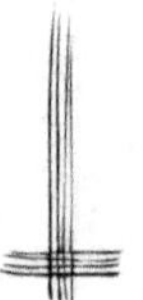

6

McKay shouldn't have been surprised at the weight of the lid, but the stone's heft was far more than he expected. He lifted it up slowly, not sure what would be inside. When nothing flashed and no cloud billowed out, he flipped the lid over and laid it delicately on a file folder.

He saw that the lid had etchings on the underside, only visible now that it was exposed.

Аббадон, Могучий.

"What is that, Russian?"

While he waited for another translation, he let his fingertips run over the other markings. *Descendit procella,* this one read. *Latin again?*

There was one more etching, which McKay had seen before. It had been on the raised altar at the compound.

Отец возник.

"Somebody get me a fucking translation on this shit, right fucking now!"

McKay was sweating through his shirt, the moisture running down his sides, pooling at the top of his ass crack.

Finally, Officer Lickman held his phone out to McKay.

"Alright, let's see here. The Russian part reads *'Abbadon, the Mighty.'* Followed by *'blackness descends'* in Latin. And this last part, also in Russian. *'Father arise.'* So, if we read the front and back side as one sentence, we have a stone lid that reads *'For a new world would come. Abbadon, the Mighty. Blackness descends. Father arise.'* Jesus fucking Christ. What the fuck is this? Everybody out!"

Once the small office had been cleared and McKay was left alone, he slumped in his chair and stared at the carvings of the humans on their knees, arms outstretched. *Fucking sheep*, he thought.

Why is it always these mindless sheep? These people who should know better, who get hooked into these religious cults and then leave me a goddamned bloody mess to clean up after?

McKay didn't even want to look in the box. He'd caught a glimpse of a dark material, most likely a wooden box, when he'd opened the lid, but now he felt drained.

His hand throbbed where the nail had impaled him. He looked at the bandage, surprised to find no red tinge of leaking blood.

He was going to lean forward, build up some courage to dig deeper into the stone box, when the rain picked up in intensity, grabbing his attention.

McKay stood and looked outside. He hadn't even realized the weather had taken such a turn. He was pissed, as he'd planned on walking home. McKay smirked at the thought. He planned on walking home yesterday. He hadn't planned on spending the night or the ER trip, but now here he was. Going on thirty-six hours at the office.

A soft knock at the door stole his eyes from the window.

"Yeah?"

"McKay, sorry to do this man, but we got a call and Sarge says he needs you to do prelim on the scene. You won't be primary, but everyone else is out and they need a detective ASAP."

He looked at the box, then back to the cop.

"Fuck. OK. Give me a sec and I'll get the details from dispatch."

The box would have to wait.

He grabbed his jacket from the hanger on the back of the door, slipping it on. He flipped his light out, taking one last look at the carved stone on his desk, then closed the door behind him, making sure to test that it was locked.

WHEN HE FINALLY RETURNED TO the precinct the box was the furthest thing from his mind. He'd been at the scene far longer than expected, and after handing the keys to the officer at auto, he knew he needed to head home.

"I'm going to get some sleep," he muttered to the officer sitting at the nearest desk. "I'll get the paperwork done up later." The officer said something to him, but he was in a haze now, exhaustion finally grasping control of his brain.

McKay waved at the cop on duty at the intake desk, before stepping outside into the deluge from above. In his office he hadn't heard any thunder or lightning, but now outside the air hummed with the expectation of the next strike.

He'd always been anti-umbrella. Just the thought of holding a stick with a tent above his head made him grimace. On this walk home, he wished he was using one.

The drops were fat and solid, falling with enough speed to sting and make him wince a few times. He hadn't even crossed the street and he was soaked, his jacket offering little defense against the volume of liquid coming from the clouds.

The light changed and he briskly crossed, not wanting to run, but annoyed enough to speed walk.

McKay cut down through the alley between the Chinese food place and the Tattoo shop.

He was halfway down the span when he came to a halt.

It wasn't raining in the alley.

McKay looked to the clouds and saw the sky was still dark, but there was no rain falling here. There was nothing covering the alley or blocking the space.

For whatever reason, the rain wasn't coming down.

He decided not think too hard on this weather phenomena and just to keep hurrying home.

It was near the end of the far side of the alley that a noise caught his attention. He felt his palm begin to pulse, where the nail had invaded his flesh.

It was the sounds from an animal's hoof, clicking and clacking on the cement behind him.

McKay refused to turn. The sound behind him striking the deepest fear in his heart he'd ever experienced.

A new sound echoed, similar to nails on a chalkboard.

He knew then.

McKay knew if he turned, he'd come face to face with the horned beast that was on the lid of the stone box. It would be ten feet tall, two massive horns curling from its goat head. It would be dragging its clawed hands against each building on either side of the alley, walking purposefully towards the detective.

He could even hear it breathing, the snort and huff from its snout.

When the sound stopped mere feet behind him, the rain began again.

McKay ran faster than he'd ever run in his life when the creature behind him whispered '*Father arise.*'

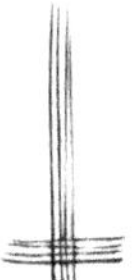

He flopped onto his bed and let his arms splay out to his sides. He stared at the ceiling fan spinning around as it *whomped whomped* slowly.

McKay kicked his shoes off. He was drenched from the storm, which was still raging outside.

Now that he was home, McKay felt foolish.

Fucking overactive imagination, he told himself. *Too many long days without sleep.*

There had been nothing in that alley. It had been a cat. Someone had tossed some garbage out from a store. He kept running these scenarios through his mind, but he knew for certain there had been no demon stalking him. The rain had kept falling, it was just his eyes playing tricks on him.

He flexed his hand, wincing with how sore it was. That piece of rusted metal had done a number on his palm. McKay wasn't too fond of the tetanus shot he'd had either.

I need to change out of these wet clothes, he thought, *turn off that fucking fan.*

Exhaustion won.

The storm grew as his eyes fell heavy and he drifted off to sleep.

Outside, on the grass, a figure pointed towards his darkened window.

McKay woke with a start, covered in sweat and still unnerved from his trip home. He was breathing heavily; his dream frightening but immediately forgotten once his eyes popped open.

The room was pitch black, the storm outside continuing even as night arrived.

He found his cell phone on the nightstand and pushed the side button, the screen illuminating.

9:00 pm.

Jesus, I've slept for almost twelve hours, he realized.

McKay saw some text notifications and a few missed calls. One jogged his memory. Missed call from Freddy. That'd be about the mystery woman. They could all wait. His body was telling him that he needed to piss and then crawl back into bed, this time under the sheets. More sleep was on the agenda.

He sat up and stared at the far side of the room.

It was immeasurably black. Normally his dresser sat

there. Even at night the hardware on each drawer would reflect some of the light from the street lights outside.

Everything churned when he realized that within the black, a figure was materializing.

"Who's there?" he asked. His voice cracked, and he sounded defeated in a way he'd never believed possible before.

The room shifted before him, the void fading away, returning his room to its normal configuration. The corner was still dark, but McKay knew someone was sitting there.

"McKay," a husky voice replied. He recognized it immediately as the woman who'd assaulted him.

"How'd you get in here?"

"An attractive woman is in your room and that's your question?"

"You stabbed me and broke my nose last time," he replied.

She laughed, the sound forcing his dick to twitch. It was the sound of someone you've just paid to fuck and they now saw you as the most charming person ever. While his bottom half betrayed him, his mind was racing. This wasn't good. He needed to get his revolver from his nightstand.

"I'm not here to kill you, McKay. I'm here to open your mind and give you more insight into what you've been thrust into."

She stood, her red silk dress falling away from her curvy figure.

McKay was losing the battle. Her aroma, even from a distance, was intoxicating.

The air bristled.

She was now standing directly before him, and just as

quick as she'd impaled him, she grabbed his head and pushed it between her breasts.

He'd lost the battle.

She pushed him back, his fall to the mattress making him feel like he was as light as a feather. Instead of taking off his pants, McKay watched her crawl up his body until she straddled his chest.

"You were never meant to be a part of this. Now, you've begun to ask questions about an incident where no answers can be found. You will learn more about events in the past when you examine that package in your office. For now, let's give you a taste of what you've stumbled upon."

She put one knee on either side of his head and before he could resist, McKay felt her pussy smash into his mouth. His tongue eagerly started to lick, his teeth and lips nibbling her folds. Her pubic hair pressed into his nose, which he breathed deeply. McKay didn't know what he expected, but the smell was earthy and invigorating. As she rode his face harder and faster, she began to moan and tremble. His nose throbbed and ached, the mangled cartilage screaming at the pressure.

McKay felt a gush of fluid spurting forth from her. It was thick and filled his mouth, flowing onto his chin and cheeks. He was expecting it to be sweet or ammonia tinted, but instead he recognized the metallic bite of blood. He struggled to push her off, but she was too strong, and instead she began to grind his face harder.

She grabbed his hair, and while she pushed down harder, she pulled his head upwards. He was locked into place. But for some reason, he kept licking.

His eyes burst wide when he felt it.

A new weight had joined them on the bed. McKay

couldn't see anything because this nude goddess was on his face.

Then he heard a gruff breath. His zipper was lowered and his pants undone. They were roughly yanked down his legs, his cock bobbing around once exposed.

Before he could try and kick this unseen intruder, McKay felt his dick engulfed into their mouth and when it bit down on the base of his shaft, a bright light exploded through his head.

Proverbs 27:20
Hell and Destruction are never full; so the eyes of man are
never satisfied.

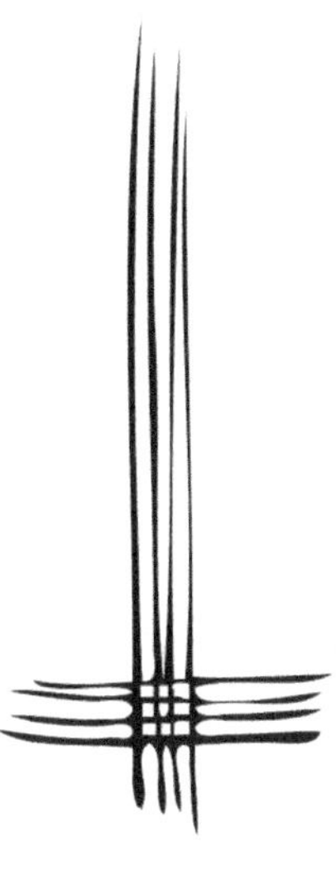

1929

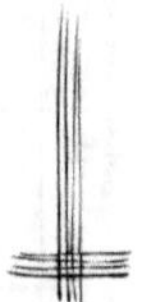

Father stood before his congregation, smiling.

He now knew the truth. The beast had told him to collect some of the discarded remains when Preacher's Rock had exploded.

Looking at the headless bodies before him, his cheeks ached from how hard he smiled.

The black veil had been lifted from his eyes.

Ascension was possible. He'd seen it when he collected the stone.

The black heavens were *above* and *beyond*.

Here and *there*.

In order to go forth and complete the ritual, he'd require a new flock.

This time one dedicated to the cause. It was clear from Nathaniel's failure that they were not pure of sin.

He'd begin recruiting in the morning.

Until then, he had to start carving the stone, forming it into its true purpose.

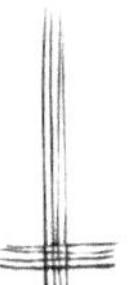

The thing Father always found interesting about humans, was that as a whole the majority were unintelligent. So, when a man wearing a robe walked into town, asking the people on the sidewalks if they had a moment to discuss religion, it only took him three days and he had one hundred new members that were planning on moving to the base of Preacher's Rock by the weekend.

He was exhilarated, when he returned to the complex.

To prepare for their arrival, he needed to dispose of all of the remains still scattered around the grounds.

While the bodies had been stacked and burned from the area near the campfire, the beast had also beheaded the parishioners who had remained in their tents and huts.

Once every residence had been cleaned and blessed, Father felt a weight leave his chest.

He would greet them one by one.

He would catalog all of the men, women and children.

Then he would choose a man and a woman to fulfill his needs and begin the next phase towards immortality.

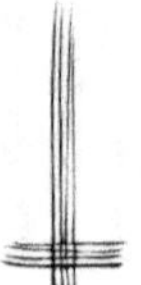

It had been a month since the compound had been re-populated.

While the initial few weeks had seen some growing pains, Father was now pleased with how well the group interacted. They all had learned their jobs, their new roles.

Leaving your old life behind was tough, he knew, but for the betterment of their chances to transcend the black realm and join their gods above, each person needed to accept their position and do it with vigor.

Each night, after final prayer and the group had dispersed back to their sleeping quarters, Father would retrieve a lantern and his walking stick and make the quarter mile hike to the base of Preacher's Rock.

The instructions had been clear. He needed to follow them to the exact specifications if he was to achieve his ultimate goal.

He was ready to determine who would need to take his seed, who would carry his child. For this to occur the stars would tell him through his sacrifice.

On this night, he sat at the base of a leafless tree and silently cut eleven thin strips of skin from the inside of his thighs. Once they had all been removed, he laid them on a flat rock before him, and meditated while looking to the sky.

After some time, his eyes lit up as the stars twinkled in such a way that he knew it was a message. He closed his eyes and let the beast speak to him.

He picked up ten of the pieces and swallowed them whole.

Turning the eleventh piece over he stared at the thin lines of blood left behind.

They spelled out a name.

He smiled as he stood, his thighs stinging from the wounds.

As he returned back to the compound, the blood made a squelching noise as he shuffled along.

The sensation of the fluid dripping down his legs made him harder than he'd been in some time.

For the next week, Father watched her.

When they had Morning Prayer, afternoon study and danced around the fire at night, he watched.

He'd sit off to the side, one hand tucked under his robe, slowly moving it along the rough skin of his penis. He knew he needed to walk that fine line for the rest of the week. He needed to be close, edged to the extreme so that when their union was consummated, the gods above and below would experience his release.

The men all clapped as the women danced and circled the flickering fire light. Her eyes caught his as she came around, and she smiled.

Father caught the red glow within her, saw her blonde hair twirl and fall, and knew the time was upon him when the clawed hand rested on his shoulder.

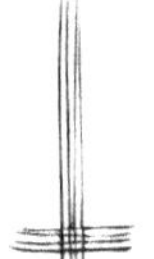

The next day, Father led them in their Morning Prayer. He conducted a sermon where he focused on helping thy fellow neighbour and ensuring that each member went above and beyond to fulfill the prophecy.

He'd yet to fully explain to them what they would attempt to be doing. He didn't want to overwhelm the group.

Soon they'd need to understand that they served a higher purpose.

While he spoke, he made sure to make direct eye contact with her. She smiled and licked her lips slowly, pulling her bottom lip in a bit and biting it with her teeth.

Father had no doubts now. The stars had spoken that evening.

To him and to her.

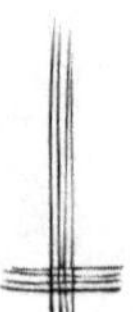

He approached her that afternoon, watching her coyly catch his gaze, smile then look away. Her beauty was ageless. A man as holy as he should find no attraction for procreation, yet she pushed him to toss away his ideals.

He took her hand, pulled her close, pressed his engorged groin into her stomach.

"Lily," he whispered, her head buried in his long, grey beard.

"Yes, my love," she replied, moving her hand lower to grab him.

"The heavens I crave have spoken to me. They've signalled that it is you to bring forth a child."

"I know, my love. The horned one has spoken to me, in my dreams."

This surprised the man. He hadn't expected her to be receptive.

"Tonight, we meet."

He shoved her down, watching her face change from lust to shock as she hit the ground.

Father spun and departed, not caring if her feelings had been hurt.

He wasn't making love to a woman. He was fulfilling his duty to bring the opening one step closer.

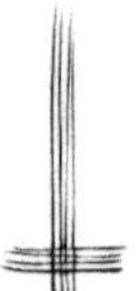

14

s dusk arrived, she was summoned.

She followed a fire-lit path through the desert, leading away from the compound.

The sky was clear, which helped lower her anxiety.

She stepped forth from the path into a small clearing at the base of a hill. She knew this hill used to be home to Preacher's Rock at the summit.

Now, she found Father standing before her, candles lit in a circle around him.

He stood nude, his body frail, his inner thighs bloody.

His member bobbed before him. Red, swollen and fixated on her.

Father wore a mask that covered his face from the nose up.

One long horn protruded from his forehead and extended back behind his head. Two tusks sprouted from each cheek and came to a point before his face.

"Lily, come. Please."

She walked within arms distance, calmer than expected.

So close to Father now, she was shocked at how little there was of him. The robe he wore disguised his skeletal figure beneath. She could see his ribs protruding, and his skin was thin to the point of being translucent. Blue veins crossed over most of his tissue.

Father took her hand and squeezed it, smiling at her from below the mask.

He deftly reached out and slipped her robe off, leaving her nude.

She kneeled before him, keeping her eyes fixed on his, the mask shrouding them. As she went to take him in her mouth, he pushed her away.

She fell back, parting her legs. As he knelt down between them, the candles all snuffed out and around the area she now heard snorts and grunts.

As Father entered her, thrusting hard, she heard steps come closer, and saw the glint of eyes within the night.

The gods were watching.

She raised her knees, letting the old man pound deeper, and when she looked at the moon and saw it flicker and go black, she knew he was about to climax.

Father confirmed her thought with a guttural noise. His cock thickened, threatening to split her from the inside. The pain was terrifyingly desired. She watched in horror as his face distorted, taking the form of the beast on the mask. His chest and arms grew wide and darkened, thick fur sprouting before disappearing.

As he finished spurting deep within, he returned to his shrivelled state, the mask falling from his head, clanging against the dirt ground.

A voice spoke from the dark, *"It is done."*

The candles danced back to life and she found that

Father stood before her, his robe back on and his walking stick in one hand.

"The consecration has occurred. You will be bathed and lathered in the days and months until the arrival. Please, follow me."

He helped her to her feet and she was surprised that none of his seed leaked out. It was as though an internal presence had lapped it up, absorbed it as soon as it entered her.

She walked behind him, nude and sore.

When they returned to the complex, two women met them, covered her in a thin robe, and led her to a hut near Father's sleeping quarters.

Once she entered, Father made his way to an area he kept hidden from the others, a small alcove behind the chapel.

There he disrobed, grabbed a cat-o-nine tails, and began to whip himself across his back and sides as he prayed for forgiveness for the act he'd committed, and for what was to come.

She could feel it grow and develop immediately.

Nothing was natural about her pregnancy. Within weeks, her stomach grew and bulged and before long she could feet the patter of little feet kicking her insides.

Father only came to visit once a week, and when he did, he wouldn't make eye contact. He would ask the midwives how things were progressing, and leave.

Each day was the same routine. Her stomach was slathered in lotions and creams and she was fed better than the group.

At night she heard the sound of a knife being sharpened on a whetstone.

Three months from conception, Lily woke in agony.

She screamed in pain as the little one in her stomach bashed and crashed, determined to make its way to the outside world.

"It's time," a female's voice said.

Lily looked over and saw a woman shrouded in a hooded robe.

She'd never seen this woman before.

"Who are you? What are you doing here?" Lily demanded, but fell silent when an immense figure loomed over their shoulder.

She couldn't make out its details, just a shape, but she knew this was one of the beasts that had watched Father and her under the rock.

Two more hooded women joined them, and as Lily was held down, Father entered her sleeping area.

He never made eye contact with Lily, instead retrieving the knife that had been sharpened nightly, and ran it across both of his palms. As the blood began to leak from his hands, he knelt, and before she could react, slid the knife across her lower abdomen. As her amniotic sac flopped out, the child still within, Father smeared the congealed mixture of fluids and tissue all over his face.

A noise beside her grabbed her attention. She glanced to her right and as she did, felt a stabbing pain in the middle of her forehead as a nail was impaled into her frontal lobe.

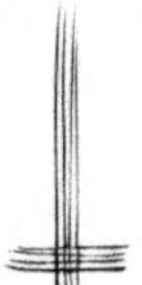

17

The tiny redheaded child grew big and strong quickly. Her assigned midwives and wet nurses made sure she was cared for and nurtured.

They kept Lily in a tent near the back of the complex, away from the other residents. She wandered the hillside behind the community for years, mouth open and drool dribbling down the sides of her chin.

Her eyes never focused, never locked onto a specific thing.

Father had no remorse or guilt over her earthly vegetative state.

He knew she'd already ascended to the black heavens.

Her role in creating their daughter was complete.

Her reward was immortality in the cosmos.

Job 10:22
The land of gloom and chaos,
Where light is like darkness.

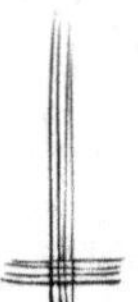

McKay screamed back into consciousness.

He looked around his bedroom, finding it bright, the sun shining outside.

The storm had moved on.

McKay expected to see the redheaded woman still sitting in the chair in the corner.

Instead he was alone.

His hand throbbed in agony, his head pounding from the punishment his nose and face had received over the last few days.

McKay sat on the edge of the bed, covered in his blanket. He didn't want to take the blanket off. He knew below would be *things* he didn't want to see or accept.

There were different aches and pains, but the part he was struggling with the most was his rational mind. None of this should be possible.

McKay counted to three in his head, and pulled the blanket aside.

His thighs were cut to shreds. He could see where skin

had been peeled back and removed, the muscle gleaming below. Eleven strips missing.

While his cock was still attached to his body, deep, dark bite wounds surrounded the base of his shaft and his balls were covered in blood. He was surprised that they still hung below, as the pain made him believe they'd been removed.

McKay found his footing and dared to stand. The room spun for a moment, but nothing worse than a few of the nights he'd drank himself into a stupor.

He shuffled to the bathroom, forcing himself to flick on the light and wait for his eyes to adjust to the brightness. Once done, he stepped before the mirror to look at the monster staring back at him.

His nose was pushed to one side, the nostrils packed with darkened, dried blood accompanied with fresh, running through it.

His lips, chin and cheeks were also caked with dark redness.

McKay didn't have a clue how he'd get cleaned up. He couldn't step into the shower to let the water wash it all away, it would sting and burn his eviscerated thighs. But he also couldn't wash his face off with one bandaged hand. The pain that any pressure would cause would be off the charts. He was fucked either way. So, he rummaged through his drawers, finding two elastic tensor bandages. McKay wrapped them around each thigh; tight but gentle. After that was done, he twisted the shower knob and waited until the water had warmed up to a tolerable heat. He stepped in with his back facing the spray, then slowly turned, allowing his face to get used to some of the pressure from the water.

It was excruciating at first, but after some time, he let the water cascade over his broken-down body. The tensor wraps did their jobs, with only a few moments of stinging pain. He wet a washcloth and delicately used it to scrub the dried blood from the rest of his face, leaving his nose for the shower nozzle alone.

McKay had to step out of the shower twice to look at his face, only to return and let the water rinse away more blood.

Finally, with only some dried gobs still around his nostrils, he turned the water off and used a towel to dry himself. He took his time on his face, dabbing and wincing as he went. He'd not bothered to wash his hair, but the motion of moving the towel back and forth on his scalp caused his eyes to water as his nose was jostled.

Once dry, he left the washroom and returned to sitting on his bed. He knew he should go back to emergency, get a once over and his legs stitched up, but the vision he'd seen when that lady had forced herself on his face was too much to ignore. McKay hadn't expected to learn what he'd learned, and he had to inspect that box sitting on his office desk more.

It was then that he saw the wall across from his bed. Last night it had been a large black void, but now in its normal state of just being a wall, long, thick scratch marks covered it from floor to ceiling.

In the middle, carved out in thick block letters, was one word.

FATHER.

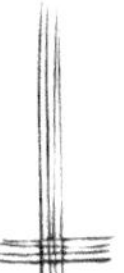

It took McKay a considerable amount of time to get dressed. He decided to change the wet tensor wraps on his legs, replacing them with clean, dry ones. When he'd undone the first one, he found it hurt like fuck to take it off, the sticky gore below clinging to the bandage.

Once he deemed his appearance acceptable, he called for a cab and waited in front of his place. McKay didn't smoke, but a part of him wished he did, longing for something in his hand, something to relax him.

He kept scanning the area, looking at the bushes and shadows nearby, expecting to see something hiding in wait.

"Hey, fella? You call for a cab?"

The cab driver startled him, so lost in thought and worry that he hadn't even heard it pull up.

The man honked now, frustration showing.

"Yeah. Yes, sorry," he said, trying to walk normally to the cab.

It hurt getting into the low vehicle, having to bend down and slide over on the seat.

When he got dropped off in front of the precinct, the officers outside of the building saw him and hustled over, helping him get out of the cab.

"Jesus, McKay? What the fuck happened?"

"You wouldn't believe me," he replied, making his way to his office.

He felt every set of eyes on him as he shuffled across the work floor.

McKay struggled to get the office unlocked, then when successful, pushed the door open and had to step back.

A smell like rot and sulphur exploded out, causing the officers nearby to rush and open the windows.

"Didn't smell like that when you left," one mentioned.

"No, no it did not."

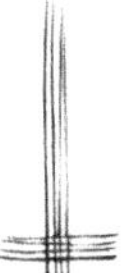

McKay shut the door behind him and sat at his desk, his chair feeling infinitely more comfortable than the cab seat had been.

He needed some time to process the events thus far. Catalog what he could. Make notes. Procedural stuff. He was still struggling with how implausible this entire thing seemed. McKay needed to focus on the normal, the mundane and routine.

Since Kramer had decided to take his own life, it had been one odd occurrence after another and if there was one thing a career of being a detective had taught him, it was to look for the pattern.

So, ignoring the box and the stench permeating the air, McKay went to his large white board and wiped it clean. He started off at the top, jotting down what he had seen in the vision. Father at the top, then Lilly, followed by the redhead child with an arrow to the right and the words 'mystery woman' beside it.

Below, he made two branches; the first for Abaddon, he'd

need to research this. He put in a call for someone to get a biblical expert to come immediately. The second branch was for Brad. He didn't understand how this random male – one that through interviews he'd determined was quite possibly the most boring man in the world – had been deemed a chosen figure to lead a ritual.

By the time he'd made a few inconsequential other notes, a knock on the door got his attention.

Turning he saw a man who looked similar to himself. Late 40's to early 50's. Tailored suit, grey black hair combed to one side.

"Can I help you?"

"I'm Professor Bianchi. I received a call and was instructed that a Detective McKay had some questions in an investigation regarding a biblical issue?"

"Fuck. That was fast."

"I was actually just down the street leaving court where I'd been testifying as an expert witness. Two-minute walk."

McKay nodded, and motioned at the chair across his desk. "Please, sit."

The professor sat and set his briefcase on his lap, which he popped open and pulled out a slim laptop. It was only then that he spotted the stone box on the desk before him. His face dropped, eyes growing wide, coloring disappearing.

"Where the fuck did you get Abaddon's heart?"

McKay just stared at the man. He'd gone from together and professional to undone in moments. He'd not expected that from a man who'd been called as an expert witness.

"Abaddon's heart?"

"Abaddon is both a place and an entity. A bottomless pit but also the king of the locusts. The bringer of plagues.

Abaddon is often accompanied by Sheol – also a place and an entity."

Sheol. McKay made a note on the whiteboard, referencing the group that had opened fire while chanting that word.

"Interestingly, the name has a number of translations. The entity has been referred to as 'the destroyer,' 'the angel of death' as well as 'doom' or 'to perish.' This entity has also been linked to the prophecy of 'The Black Heavens.' In some cult sects, the black heavens are the astrological or cosmic location of immortality."

Now McKay's own expression change. This professor seemed to be giving him all of the information he needed, without even being prompted. Normally he'd be suspicious of something like this, but after what he'd experienced, he knew better.

"So, Abaddon's heart is what?"

Bianchi leaned in closer, examining the sides of the stone as well as the lid on top. Even though his initial reaction had been deep fear, he was nevertheless showing excitement over what was sitting before him.

"Sorry, would you mind if I took some pictures of this? This is extraordinary to just stumble on this in person."

"Have at it. There's something under the lid I can show you when you're done on the outside. Then can you answer me?"

"Yes, yes," he said, quickly retrieving his cellphone and pulling up the camera app.

Once he was done taking his photos of the side and top, McKay flipped the lid over and let him inspect the under surface. He purposefully blocked the box inside. He hadn't yet inspected this and didn't want to disclose something unintentionally.

"OK, all done?"

Bianchi nodded, returning to the seat.

"Alright, Abaddon's heart. In my circles you hear stories within the collector's world, the black market of artifacts. A number of us who are... more open to working within this world of collector's, know of its origins. The story goes that Abaddon, was banished to the underworld. While there, the entity was slain by the sword of an unknown soldier. The heart was removed and placed inside a box."

He stopped here and eyed McKay. McKay realized Bianchi had been expecting to be interrupted. The subject matter was such that he'd probably been interrupted before.

"Well, we hear nothing of the box for some time. There are rumblings of it being used in various rituals, or of many of the immoral Popes using it to speak to God, but it just disappears from the record. Sure, we see some documents suggesting it was transported to Russia where the mad monk, Rasputin was privy to it. Some believe he successfully contacted Abaddon, and he himself ascended to the black heavens."

This would explain the languages on the box, McKay thought.

"Is that the end of the story?" McKay asked.

"No. We get some time again where information goes dark. The last I'd heard of the box was that it was seen in France. So, from France, to your desk. Now, here it sits."

McKay had to sit and stare at the box before him. While he couldn't fathom all that Bianchi stated, it did paint a vivid picture. One that he could see related to this Father character, who was so hell bent on this prophecy and promise of immortality he'd do whatever it took.

"What is the purpose of all of this? Of the Abaddon heart?"

"Detective. The purpose is that it is a direct line to Abaddon. That what is stored in the box not only relates to the entity as well as the location, but that it also allows communication with the beast. That is, if the ritual is done correctly and favour is received."

"Favour?"

"Yes. An entity such as Abaddon is something that will only do something in return. A favour for a favour. A ritual must be performed. The documents I've seen have all said that those who've tried to summon this beast have had to ensure every single thing is done perfectly, and without pause or fail, for Abaddon to be pleased and to open up the black void. Allow a human to step into the black heavens."

McKay felt his blood run cold. *Black void? Like in his bedroom?*

"May I ask a question, Detective McKay?"

McKay nodded, unsure what would be asked.

"Is there a wooden box within this stone box?"

McKay didn't want to answer the man. He wanted none of this to be happening. Hearing all of this backstory, his thighs throbbed and his hand itched.

"There is."

Bianchi nodded.

The two sat silently, contemplating what that meant.

Finally, Bianchi took the lead.

"Have you looked inside?"

"I have not."

"May I ask, is this box related to your appearance?"

"It is."

"I think, for me to have a better understanding of what my role can be for you, I'd like you to fill me in please."

McKay filled him in.

On everything.

Starting from his deceased partner going to visit Father and his flock, up until Bianchi had knocked on his office door. He left nothing out, not even the visit by the woman and the events that occurred. McKay told him every detail he could of the vision, and even what had happened to him physically.

It felt good to get it off of his chest, but at the same time he was now concerned about Bianchi leaking any of these details.

Once done, Bianchi took a few minutes. He stared at the stone again, hands together.

"I think for me to help at all, the next step would be for me to sign an NDA."

"A non-disclosure agreement?"

"Yes. I need to make sure you are completely honest with me. Someone in your position will be worried that I might take the info and run. We need to trust each other. We need to open that box and for you to know that I will not share anything that we've discussed. I would, however, like to email these photos to a trusted colleague to get their opinion on what it is we are looking at. I'm very confident, but a second opinion is best."

"Absolutely. Go ahead. I'll get that NDA here within ten minutes."

McKay made a call and then the two waited for it to arrive.

Both knew that once Bianchi signed the document, they'd open up the box.

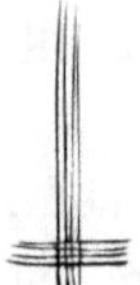

Outside a new storm moved in.

The sky was dark and angry.

The clouds opened and the rain drops began slamming to the ground.

People walking along the sidewalks took cover.

At first, they thought it was just rain, but the buzzing of locusts in the distance created a fear all on its own.

23

Once Bianchi signed the forms, McKay opened his bottom drawer, took out two shot glasses and put them on the desk. He grabbed a small bottle from the drawer, filled both glasses, and replaced the bottle.

McKay handed one to the professor and lifted the other before him.

They touched glasses and drank the liquor in one shot.

Once the glasses were set to the side, McKay got up and closed the office door, and flipped the blinds closed.

"Shall we?"

Bianchi nodded.

McKay found he was breathing heavy, sweat dripping down his forehead and stinging his eyes and nose.

His nose had thankfully stopped bleeding, but the little cuts and scrapes let him know it was still as fucked up as he remembered it.

Every time he moved, he grimaced.

The two stood, staring down at the stone box.

The beast carved in the top stared back, almost daring them to go down this rabbit hole.

McKay handed Bianchi some gloves, while putting his on.

The two shared one more look, before McKay grasped the lid and pulled it off, setting it on the cabinet against the side wall.

"You haven't looked at anything in here yet?"

"No. I couldn't bring myself to do it before. Exhaustion. Fear. Not sure, but I had to wait."

"Fair enough," Bianchi replied. "How about I'll take photos and catalog each piece as you take things out? That way at least there's some formality to this process?"

"That works."

McKay took a cursory glance inside to see what was there. He reached in and took out the wooden box first. He'd almost expected a shock or a pain to occur when he made contact, but was thankful nothing happened.

"First item is a wooden box," he said to the professor. "I'd say it's eight inches deep by eight inches wide. Maybe ten inches long? There are markings on it, but the wood is too dark to see. I'll get forensics to lighten it up."

He set it beside Bianchi, who began taking pictures. Once he was done, he nodded and McKay reached in again.

"Second item is a thick Manilla envelope. Something is inside. Envelope is nine inches across by maybe a foot tall. With the stuff inside, I'd wager its three inches thick."

He set this on the desk for Bianchi to catalog.

He looked in again and saw there were two more objects. One caught his eye more than the other. He pulled it out and saw Bianchi's eyes go wide.

"Item number is three is a roll of film. Not sure of type.

Old. Looks like we'll need a projector to watch it. There is a date on the side. Very faded. It may say June or July, but the year is visible. 1979."

He set it down for Bianchi, and reached in, grabbing the last object. He pulled it out and saw it was a black sack. It had a pull cord to tighten at the top, and the material was soft and smooth. It didn't feel like leather, but was close.

"Last item. Not sure what this is. Carrying sack? There is something inside but it isn't heavy."

He set it down and Bianchi quickly snapped some more pictures on his phone.

"OK. Now let's go through each item. Let's start with the box."

McKay pulled it over and examined the outside. It looked like there were letters etched into the sides, but someone either had polished the exterior or age had distorted it. He'd let forensics deal with it.

He flipped the lid open and stared at what greeted him.

"Fuck."

Bianchi covered his mouth after swearing.

Inside the wooden box were two six-inch-long horns.

"Those can't be real, can they?"

Bianchi was talking to himself now. He stood and paced his side of the desk, muttering to himself.

McKay gently removed them both, setting them on the desk. The ends were smooth, as though they had been cut off of whatever they'd belonged to.

"The horns look like they start to curve but they were removed just before that point."

McKay heard Bianchi, but he blocked most of it out.

"Let's look in this envelope."

He unlooped the red thread that kept the envelope closed.

Once it was undone, he looked inside, not surprised to find a stack of photos.

Some were in black-and-white, while others were in color.

McKay saw that they were in some semblance of an order, so he started at the top of the stack, and analyzed each one before passing it to Bianchi, who'd now returned to sitting.

The first fifty or so photos were mundane. Boring to a degree. All were in black-and-white and all appeared to be showing daily life at the compound.

Some showed women doing laundry or making food, some showed them playing with children or teaching them various things. There were photos of them all kneeling and looking forward, McKay assumed this was them praying or attending their church. Other photos showed men making and building things, shirtless and sweaty. It spoke to the time period, McKay realized. Of women doing female chores and men doing male tasks. Most cults seemed to want to maintain that patriarchal mentality. This was similar to most religions.

It wasn't until fifty or so pictures in that McKay experienced a sharp kick to his stomach. The photo before him showed Father, standing beside a very pregnant woman. He knew that was Lily. He hadn't seen much in his vision of things like this, but he knew the vision had served a purpose. It was unsettling to look upon them as a 'couple.' They looked happy even.

The next few photos showed Father in various moments; a man knelt before him, Father touching his head with his eyes closed. Father standing on a rock above the gathered crowd, arms wide.

It wasn't until the photos turned to color that the content began to change.

Gone were the mundane scenes of life. Instead, McKay was looking at true horror.

The first photo showed a woman with blood covering her hands sitting under a tree. Beside her sat what McKay assumed were intestines. He wasn't sure as the photo was blurry, but the ropey viscera possessed a distinct shape, one McKay had seen far too many times on the job. A body hung from a branch beside where she sat, their stomach splayed open and empty.

In the next one, Father stood nude while a man was kneeling before him. Father held a hammer high above the man. In the next photo, a man lay on the ground with a bloody hammer sticking out of his skull.

The next few photos displayed some men and women nude. Each were bound to a wooden cross. Long, red marks criss-crossed their fronts and backs. Father stood near them with a whip in his hand.

It was evident from the photos that Father was becoming more and more depraved and hurtful. Angry.

It was near the back of the stack that McKay found the most interesting photos. Some were showing a circle of candles in the dirt, Father standing with his robe pulled open, long cuts bleeding on his chest.

Others showed a robed man, wearing a mask with horns, pouring red liquid from a cup over crying babies.

These images got to McKay. He'd seen a lot of fucked up shit in his career, experienced things and witnessed events that humans shouldn't. Even the visit hadn't affected him like this. These innocent children were simply playthings in Father's quest for immortality.

He set the photos aside, giving himself a breather. He asked Bianchi if he wanted a coffee, and excused himself to get them each a cup.

When he returned, Bianchi was still jotting down notes related to each photo before him.

"Thanks," the professor said, taking a sip before setting it on the desk.

McKay picked the stack up, feeling a bit better.

The next few photos were startling.

While out of focus and blurry, as though the photographer was either moving or trying to be stealthy, they each showed something McKay didn't believe he'd ever see.

The first was a photo of a woman strapped to a chair. She was covered in blood. Father stood to her side, holding a knife. Behind the chair, at the edge of the darkness, was the outline of a large figure. McKay could swear that he could see red eyes, hooves, and twisted horns on top of its head.

The next few were similar. A male bound nude over a log, Father pressed up behind the man, robe thrown back. The male's head had a clawed hand placed on it, the owner of the hand just off camera.

McKay handed these to Bianchi and waited for the man to get to them. When he did, he jumped up, chair pushed back, toppling over and hitting the ground.

"It can't be," he said, pointing at the picture.

The professor crossed himself and exited the office, walking across the work floor without looking back.

While he waited for his return, McKay flipped through the last dozen photos. These were simple ones, nothing really of note. It was a stark change in subject matter. Members all dancing around a campfire, a woman sitting with a few children.

The last photo caught his attention.

It was a Polaroid.

It was of two boys and a girl sitting at a table. The first boy was young, maybe five. The second boy was younger still, maybe two. The girl was older, she looked to be a teenager.

The date said "May 13th, 1992."

McKay felt his heart race when he stared at the girl. He knew her. It clicked into place that it was the mystery woman who had assaulted him.

The name of the girl was smudged and unreadable.

The younger of the two had nothing written under him.

The name written under the older boy was easy to read.

Brad, age five.

McKay looked in the envelope and found a piece of discarded paper left behind. Pulling it out, he read what was written on it.

'Watch the film.'

Psalm 143:3
For the enemy has pursued me,
crushing my life to the ground,
making me sit in darkness like those long dead.

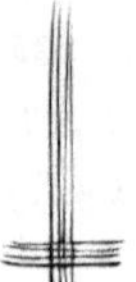

It was as though the note in the envelope was speaking to McKay from beyond.

He sent a request for a video technician, someone who could figure out what type of film was on this reel and get a projector to broadcast it.

McKay contacted a colleague in another precinct to come watch.

With any video found of this nature, he wanted to ensure that what was seen the first time would not be doctored and manipulated if this was to be used in court. This way his colleague could verify the authenticity of what was shown on the film. They'd send it to forensics to have someone verify the age, and that the film hadn't been altered after viewing it.

While they waited for McKay's colleague to arrive and the projector to be set up, they decided to order some food. Both were starving, not having realized how much of the day had gotten away from them.

After deciding on pizza, McKay was surprised when the guy at the pizza joint said it would take an hour to deliver.

"You haven't seen the storm outside?" he asked, his voice bordering on annoyance.

"No, sorry. I've been inside all day investigating a homicide."

McKay chuckled when the guy apologized and said he'd try and speed the food up. That line always got civilians.

He hit End Call and sat down, feeling the weight of everything climbing up his shoulders.

"Fuck me, I'm tired."

"You look it, no offense," Bianchi said, as he kept typing on his laptop.

McKay waved it off.

"Gonna piss."

Leaving the office, his thighs screamed with the exertion, his hand howling when he opened and closed it.

When all of this is over, I'm gonna need a massage, he thought. *A nice happy ending to relieve some stress.*

McKay pushed the door as he entered the washroom, cringing as it creaked.

He walked to the urinal, unzipped and let out a sigh as his bladder emptied.

It was then that he heard a snort and smelled rotting flesh.

He closed his eyes, finished peeing, then zipped up slowly.

McKay turned, washed his hands and then walked as fast as he could out of the washroom. He almost bumped into an officer entering, who said *watch it*, as he entered and McKay left.

He didn't hear anything. No screams of agony or sounds of a struggle.

Making his way back to his office, he found his colleague standing at the doorway waiting for him.

When Detective Grant turned and saw McKay, he didn't hide his shock.

"You weren't kidding when you said he was fucked up," Grant said to Bianchi.

"Real joker," McKay replied, grabbing a chair from an officer's desk and positioning it for Grant.

The tech arrived, quickly determining what type of film it was, and set it up on the projector.

"Good to go, McKay. Just call when you're done and I'll break the equipment down and catalog the reel."

The man left, leaving the three sitting in the office.

"You want more background on this, Grant? Other than it's related to the cult?"

"Nah. Let's go in blind."

McKay nodded, turned off the light, and flipped the switch on the side.

The machine made a clacking noise, before whirling to life.

A picture emerged on the projector screen on the far wall.

One McKay and Bianchi couldn't believe.

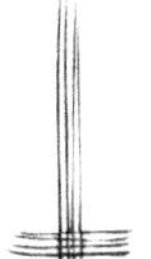

There was no sound.

The room was silent other than the whirl of the projector.

Outside the rain continued to increase in intensity.

The thunder rumbled, the lightning beginning to flash and strike.

A shrouded figure strode from between two buildings, and then stood outside on the lawn of the precinct.

They began to chant '*Sheol, Sheol,*' over and over again.

As the picture came into focus in the office and the three men saw the first image of Father sitting before the camera, the figure removed their robe.

Standing naked in the rain, they dropped to their knees, arms stretched above them.

A second figure emerged from the alley, walked briskly to the nude person and slit their throat.

They disappeared back into the blackness before any one even noticed they'd been there.

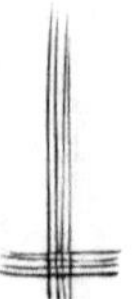

McKay, Grant and Bianchi heard a commotion outside the office, but ignored it. The film had flickered to life, Father sitting before the camera.

With no sound, it was irritating to be unable to hear what he was saying, but from what they could see it appeared he was reading something out loud.

"Who's this guy?" Grant asked.

"Father. Head of the cult."

"Whack job," Grant chuckled.

The camera angle was such that Father appeared to be addressing people behind the setup, but the camera never turned to show any group of gathered people.

It flickered and a new scene began.

This one was immediately shocking.

It showed a group of naked worshippers wearing masks, all crawling in circles on their hands and knees. As they passed Father, he would whip them, kick them or slash at them with an object. By the third trip around the man, the parishioners were bloody and even with no sound, one could see they were screaming in pain.

"Some kinky shit you two are watching," Grant said, laughing.

A new scene came on.

This one showed Father sodomizing a male. He was pumping rigorously into the male's rear while he burned the man's back with a torch he was holding. The area around them was dark, not visible to the camera, but it was within that blackness that Bianchi spotted something.

"What the fuck is that?"

He was pointing to a place on the screen to the top right.

In the area, McKay and Grant both started to see what Bianchi had spotted. Something immense and disfigured was swaying in and out of the shadows.

"Is that fucking nut job wearing a dead goats head? Perv's man," Grant joked.

"No. We believe what we are seeing is real footage of Abaddon," Bianchi replied.

"Abaddon? Like a fucking demon?"

"Entity," Bianchi was quick to point out.

"It's a fucking demon," Grant replied.

The three men watched. The faster and harder Father fucked that tortured male, the closer and closer the creature came to stepping into the light.

"I've watched enough porn to know that old man's about to blow his load," Grant said, leaning in and staring at the blackness before the creature.

"Come on, motherfucker. Step into the light." Grant was sitting right on the edge of his seat now.

On screen, Father thrust into the man one last time, then

threw his head back. From this angle, they could see he was in ecstasy.

"There it is! Holy fucking shit!"

Grant was practically jumping out of his chair as the creature stepped from the shadows.

Fully exposed, McKay inhaled hard, Bianchi matching his shock.

The creature was easily ten feet tall, filling up the side of the screen. It was standing on two hairy legs, hooves instead of human feet. The legs were bent at an unnatural angle, closer to a dog's hind legs than a human structure.

Its torso was bare, and looked like a human's stomach.

McKay wasn't sure, but he believed it had two appendages sprouting from its back, much like the membranous wing's bats possessed.

It had a goat's head with two curled horns adorning the top.

It stepped forward and with outstretched hands that finished in thick claws, ripped the man's head off and eagerly lapped at the blood that poured from the base of his neck.

The camera moved and blurred before refocusing.

The three men were stunned with what they saw next.

A thick set of ropes had been wrapped around the beast.

The parishioners were imprisoning this demon.

A knock on the door caused them all to scream.

McKay flipped off the projector and went to the door.

Opening it, he saw a frazzled pizza guy standing there.

"Oh, shit. Sorry. Completely forgot," McKay said, fishing for his wallet.

"Sorry it took so long, mister. That'll be $20. That dead person out front really made it tough to get in here."

"Dead person," McKay quizzed, not sure what the guy meant.

"Yeah. Wait? Didn't you see? Someone killed themselves on your guy's front lawn."

McKay handed the pizza box to Bianchi and went to the window, looking out. Sure enough a scene had been taped off, and a sheet covered a body.

"Well fuck. No, we've been focused in here."

He handed the guy two twenties and then shut the door. He didn't need the change and knew the tip would be appreciated.

"I say we eat, take a minute and then watch whatever the fuck is next," McKay suggested.

"Sounds good. You got any booze?" Grant asked.

"Bottle in the drawer," McKay replied.

While Grant got the bottle and started to slug it back, McKay looked at Bianchi giving him a '*what the fuck*' look.

"This is extraordinary," Bianchi said. "Just stunning. I think I know what will happen next, but I can't believe this is on film."

"I gotta say, I wasn't expecting to come watch freaky demon porn with you two fucks, but the special effects are impressive on this flick," Grant said.

McKay nodded, surprised at how delicious the pepperoni tasted. He was famished, and this cheese and meat slice of dough was hitting the spot perfectly.

THEY FINISHED EATING, Grant and Bianchi used the washroom, and they all got situated, ready to see this film out.

"Ready?"

Both nodded to McKay. He flipped the switch back on and they heard the whirl of the projector.

The screen flickered and twitched before the reel caught and the scene returned to life.

Now, they watched as the creature came into view.

It was struggling and roaring, the sound close to crossing the years and the void.

"Jesus, fuck," Grant said to himself. Bianchi stared at the footage, face blank and expressionless.

They watched as Father approached the creature, and

when he was beside it, he turned and spoke. The camera twisted and showed a gathering of people, all pushed in close.

The camera returned to Father, who motioned with his hands. Three men and three women approached, disrobed and knelt before the creature and the man.

Father reached behind the chair the beast was bound on and produced a handsaw.

When McKay and Bianchi saw that, they both turned to look at the two pieces of six-inch horn sitting on the desk. Grant saw them turn, so he followed their heads to see what they were looking at.

"Fuck no. Fuck off. Seriously?" he said, scrambling to his feet. He moved away from the desk but continued watching the footage.

As Father sawed back and forth, first through the end of one horn and then the other, the six people kneeling before the beast were chanting something. Bianchi was trying to read their lips.

"Sheol. That's what they're chanting. They are summoning the underworld," he finally said.

A redheaded woman appeared, McKay recognizing her immediately.

She walked before each of the kneeling people, and slit their throats one at a time.

When the six had fallen, she turned and kneeled before the beast.

Father finished cutting the horns off. One done with that, he reached down to the crotch of the beast and produced its penis.

The woman leaned in and while she began to perform fellatio on the beast, Father stabbed the creature in the chest with a long, sharp object. McKay's hand throbbed. Father started cutting away a section of its left breast.

McKay was transfixed. Watching the woman's head bob up and down. Watching the beast strain and writhe, trying to break free. Watching the rhythmic way in which Father cut the section of the beast.

When he'd made a jagged circle in its chest, Father pulled the section of tissue away. The man appeared to punch the opening, his hand working deep inside the chest cavity.

"He's pulling out the heart," Bianchi said. McKay knew he was right.

From behind the three men, they heard a sound.

They all turned and looked, finding the source immediately.

"No fucking way," Grant said.

The soft black sack that had been in the wooden box pulsated.

"Are you fucking trying to tell me that a demon's heart is in that sack?"

McKay looked back at the footage.

The woman stood, apparently finished.

Father held something in his hand. He looked euphoric.

He dropped to his knees and took a bite from the dark thing he held.

The beast let out a bellow, its mouth gaping wide, before it slumped and ceased moving.

The three men watched as the woman brought a sack that looked identical to the one on McKay's desk and Father placed the flesh inside.

The camera followed as Father walked to a wide table

and placed the two cut pieces of horn as well as the sack inside.

The footage ended as the lid was closed.

"This is a big fucking elaborate joke, yeah? Like, you two assholes called me over here, and now I got to sit through some shitty silent movie as a joke. Right, McKay? Fuck."

The projector was still rattling around as the film had come off the spool and McKay hadn't made the effort to flip the switch. He was struggling to process a few things.

The sack was still pumping and pulsating on the desk. It was as though whatever Father had done on the screen had evoked some power and brought whatever was inside to life. McKay could feel his thighs and hand bleeding. He didn't want to look at the bandage on his palm or the tensor wraps. He knew they'd be soaked through.

He also couldn't explain why he was so aroused, to the point that he was certain if he so much as stood the pressure of his pants against his erection would cause him to ejaculate.

Grant paced the room, becoming more and more animated. Bianchi stood silently. McKay did notice it looked like the man was silently crying, tears cascading over his cheeks.

Just what the fuck had they watched?

McKay flipped the projector off, and waited until he felt safe to stand.

"I need some air," he said, neither men paying mind.

He opened the door and was greeted by an officer about to knock.

"What's up?"

"McKay, we need you outside. The incident is related to your case."

"It is?"

"Yeah, there's a few connections."

He followed the officer, caught off guard. McKay knew he looked like shit, stunk, and was as far away from appearing professional as possible. Hopefully the media presence was minimal outside or he'd get chewed out when the footage aired.

"What do we got?"

The two homicide detectives standing there turned and smirked.

"Fuck, McKay. You need to pay your girls better. That way they won't have their pimps fuck you up." They both burst out laughing but stopped when they saw McKay's face.

"I'm in no fucking mood, and now this shit out here. So, what do we got?"

McKay inspected the body, took a few notes, before following the two back inside.

It was in here that they showed him the security footage of the incident.

As soon as McKay heard the chanting, and saw the figure approach and leave, he understood how this was related.

"Send me the footage, and assign an officer to that body when it's transported."

Heading back to his office, McKay was surprised to detect something in his gut. Almost a yearning, or longing, as though the distance he'd put between himself and the sack had caused some emotional hurt.

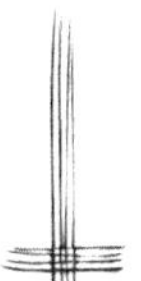

When he returned to his office, Grant had calmed down. He was sitting in his chair, hands behind his head. His armpits had soaked through from sweat, matching McKay's own shirt.

Bianchi was furiously typing away on the laptop.

Surprisingly, the sack still sat on the desk, the material rising and falling.

"You look in this?"

"Fuck no, McKay. I was waiting for you to return so I can sign whatever and get the fuck out of here. I need to go get blackout drunk so I never remember this day."

McKay slid the document to the man, who produced a pen, signed it, and left without saying a word.

"What now?"

Bianchi looked up, running McKay's question around in his brain.

"I hesitate to answer. Only because I don't believe you'll like my reply."

McKay sat, feeling his pants squish as he made contact. It wouldn't feel good when he tried to take them off later.

"Shoot."

"I think we both need some distance from this. I think we both go home, try and get some rest, and reconvene tomorrow. You said before that you were trying to determine a motive for what occurred at the cult complex? I think we've found the why. Father regretted imprisoning or eliminating the presence. The ritual performed was to bring the entity back into the flesh. They wanted to open the black heavens, but I believe Abaddon would only allow that to happen if its heart and horns were returned."

"Fuck's sake. That makes sense."

"Unfortunately, from what I've been reading here on the dark web, that would be the order of things. I suspect, and it's only a hunch, that the redheaded woman from before wanted you to see what happened, but she'll be returning for this box."

McKay knew this already. He'd suspected it from their first encounter.

"When I first met the woman, after she stabbed me, she said to go to Preacher's Rock. I'm going to head out there now. You go home, Bianchi. You've been a great help. I'll see you tomorrow."

Bianchi nodded, folded his laptop, replaced it in his briefcase and shook McKay's hand.

Once he was alone, McKay closed the door and licked his lips. He wanted to look in the pouch, see what was pulsating. But something deep inside told him to wait.

He went to auto and signed out a patrol car.

As McKay drove back to the complex, he felt that pain of distance from the sack and the horns growing once again.

Job 7:8
The eye that beholds me will see me no more;
while your eyes are upon me, I shall be gone.

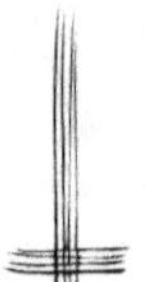

30

McKay parked his car and limped through the now abandoned commune. It had been just over a week since the mass suicide had occurred, but with the state this place looked today, it could have happened decades ago.

The blank, dark windows glared at him as he shuffled through the center of the buildings, walked by the entrance to the worship area, and proceeded to follow the path away from the dwellings. Discarded police tape fluttered haphazardly around the area.

Preacher's Rock loomed beyond the complex. It was only a short distance away, but with McKay's current condition and the sweltering heat, he felt like he had been walking for hours when he finally arrived at the base.

He immediately spotted the area from his vision, where Father had impregnated Lily. It made him feel repulsed when he thought back to that moment.

McKay didn't know what he was supposed to look for,

but he figured there was a specific reason the woman had suggested he return here.

He searched the clearing where the candles had been placed in the vision, morbidly wondering if any of the impressions on the ground were the place where Lily had lain.

McKay circled the base of the mountainous outcropping. Even in exhaustion and physical hell, his keen eyes darted back and forth. His occupation dictated he looked for the one thing that didn't belong.

It was as he was about to give up looking in this area and make the trek up the path that he caught it. A glint of something metallic reflecting deeper under an overhang.

He stooped down and shuffled to the spot. He wiped the dirt and dust away, letting his eyes fall on what reflected.

It was a marker. A simple metal arrow pointing deeper.

"Well fuck."

He pulled out his cellphone and hit the flashlight app. The overhang was more of a cave, he saw. He moved along slowly, thighs screaming, taking care not to bash his head on the rock roof.

When he made it to what he believed to be the back surface, he saw that it wasn't a rock wall at all. It was a stone slab leaning at an angle.

McKay pulled it and stepped away as it fell to the ground, hitting with a thud, throwing dust everywhere. He knew he'd never be able to lift it on his own, but he didn't care.

He looked at what now stood before him.

An opening.

An entrance to a stairwell that led down.

31

His flashlight app lit the way as he followed the stone stairs deeper under the surface.

McKay saw the telltale signs he'd expect to see in a place like this; sconces to hold lit torches, uneven steps, and the ever-growing claustrophobia of darkness above.

He no longer could make out the opening when he looked back, the light from the surface snuffed out.

Another half dozen steps and McKay came to the bottom. A chamber stretched out before him. Twenty feet by twenty feet, the light from his phone showed him that he was alone.

In the middle of the room was a slab with what looked like a sarcophagus on it.

McKay examined the walls first. Much like at a crime scene, he rarely went straight to the victim. He wanted to get an idea of the layout, the surroundings first. Look at where the incident happened before focusing on the main event.

The walls had crude carvings on them. It was hard to

make out what they were supposed to depict, but he did see some Latin and some bible verse numbers.

He didn't spend much time on them, not seeing anything of pertinent importance.

McKay made his way to the middle of the room.

Standing over the sarcophagus, he saw that there were six words etched into the top.

Lily. Ascended to the black heavens.

McKay pushed the lid as hard as he could, the weight double that of the stone slab blocking the entrance to the stairs.

His entire body screamed at him, his thighs and hand the most. Mckay's nose started to bleed from the exertion, but once the lid started to move, he didn't stop, knowing he'd never get it started again.

The lid finally slid far enough over that gravity forced it to tumble and slam to the floor.

Dust exploded out from the exposed inside, the stink of stale air and rot hitting McKay.

Looking inside, he saw why.

The mummified remains of a woman lay within.

Some sort of preservation techniques had been administered.

She was on her back, holding a skull in her hands. The skull was sitting on her stomach. In the middle of the skull's forehead was a round hole. From what McKay had been shown in the vision, he knew who that skull belonged to.

The woman, remarkably, still had skin on her body. She had a tattered robe draped around her, but most of her torso and chest was exposed. The parts of her legs he could see, were covered in thick scars.

Where the head would have been was the most unsettling.

Sitting atop the corpse was a cow's head. Its tongue had been cut off, leaving the grey mush of the remains to dangle out one side. Its eyes were glassy, somehow still full of fluid. Around its nostrils were red globs, which looked to be dried blood, but without analysis McKay was speculating. This explained the stench of rot. Someone had put this cow's head here recently.

McKay leaned in, looking closely at the necklace around the base of the body's neck. While he peered closer, he heard a soft padding sound from behind him, as though someone was approaching on bare feet.

He stiffened as the air shifted behind him.

McKay could feel breathing hitting his neck. There, gone. There, gone.

Whatever was behind him whispered then; *"Father arise."*

McKay swung around, determined to punch or grab the intruder. Finding he was still alone in the chamber did nothing to settle his nerves.

"Come on! Who's there?"

He shone the light in all directions, still coming up blank.

Seeing nothing, he returned to the corpse. Something about that necklace had caught his attention.

He reached in and delicately lifted it up so that he could see the plate that was attached to the metal loop.

"What the fuck?"

The plate read McKay.

Out of the corner of his eye he caught a subtle twitch, a movement barely perceptible.

He straightened and looked at the cow's head.

Then it blinked.

The drive back to the precinct was as much of a blur for McKay as the pained sprint from the chamber to the car.

Somehow, he ended up sitting at his desk.

All the while he had flashes of the cow's head blinking, of the whispered voice from behind him as he hustled up the stairs, and the blare of car horns as he weaved in and out of traffic.

By nightfall he was spent.

He wanted to return home, but felt safer and more grounded in the real world by remaining at the station.

While he decided on what he needed to do, he buzzed the desk of an officer working late in the work space.

Officer White hurried to McKay's office.

"You rang, McKay?"

"You were a medic in the army, right?"

"I was. Why's that?"

"I need some help, off the record. Are you willing to help with some bandages, but no report?"

"$100."

"Deal. Come in, close the door and shut the blinds please."

White did as asked, and sat on the chair.

"So, where we working on?"

"My hand and my thighs."

White's eyebrows went up.

"I heard about the crazy who stabbed your hand. It was a nail, yeah?"

White's words caused his head to spin. The room tumbled and twirled, his stomach lurching.

"Jesus, here," White said, handing the waste basket to McKay. The timing was perfect as McKay vomited into the basket.

He had been stabbed through the hand with a nail. Father had stabbed Abaddon with a long, sharp object. Most likely a nail. Lily had been lobotomized with a nail. More bile rose. He knew full well that he could never prove it, but he was positive it would be the same nail.

"Sorry," McKay mumbled, not wanting to reveal what was actually making him ill. "Haven't ate much. Blood loss as well. Just dizzy."

"Sure. You're the boss. I'm not going to argue with $100."

McKay showed him his bled-through bandage on his hand, before he stood and dropped his pants revealing the glistening red tensor bandages. A smell permeated the air.

"Fuck man. When did that happen? That smells infected."

"I think it was last night? Two nights ago? I can't actually remember. I've been burning the candle at both ends here with this case."

"Let me get some supplies. Just sit here," White said.

He returned a short time later with a fully stocked first-aid kit.

"Look, I'll clean you up and make it as pretty as I can, but you need to get some antibiotics. Infections are not something to fuck around with."

McKay nodded, and started to remove his tensor wraps.

"Fuck me," he grimaced, pain shooting up his legs as the stuck part of the tensor pulled away from his wounds.

White went to work, dabbing, wiping and dabbing some more. When all was said and done, McKay's thighs and hand were rebandaged and for a brief second the throbbing disappeared.

"Thank you."

"Any time. Now pay up," he chuckled.

McKay grabbed his wallet and handed the man two fifties.

"You need a lift home?" White asked, pocketing the cash.

"Nah. I'm going to finish some notes and I'll get a lift from someone later."

White said his goodbyes and left McKay alone.

McKay stared at the scattered debris on his desk.

It was odd. Now that he'd returned and the distance between him and the sack was so small, his pain was less.

He picked up the sack and moved his hand with the mass inside as it expanded and contracted.

Placing the sack back in the wooden box, he retrieved the two pieces of horn and put them in as well. He placed the photos into the envelope and tucked that in as well. Finally, he closed the lid and put the box back into the stone container.

McKay wiped his brow, put the stone lid back on top, before picking it up and leaving his office. He closed and locked the door behind him, before he crossed the work floor.

Dread and guilt filled him as he tried not to bring any attention to himself.

He got to the front desk, made brief small talk with the night desk clerk, then stepped outside.

The rain had stopped hours ago, but the air was damp and heavy.

Instead of getting patrol to drop him off, he decided to hail a cab.

The ride home was short.

McKay entered his house tentatively, expecting to be ambushed by the redhead.

Instead he found his home as he'd left it.

His bedroom was still in a state of disarray.

Blankets scattered, and clothes strewn about.

The weight of everything slammed down on him.

McKay set the stone box beside his bed and changed from his suit. It felt good to put on some shorts and a t-shirt after so many days of work wear.

Sitting on the bed, his thoughts drifted back to the footage, as well as what he'd seen under Preacher's Rock.

The head had blinked. His name had been on that necklace.

None of it made sense.

He felt his hand throb again, as though thinking of that hole in the skull had created a connection with his injury.

McKay couldn't fight sleep anymore.

Too many long days and longer nights.

The visit, the footage, the photos, the trip to Preacher's Rock.

It all caught up to him as sleep take over his brain.

He pulled the sheet back, content to use it as his blanket, and crawled onto the bed and experienced a release of stress as his head gently connected with his pillow. His nose reminded him to limit the pressure, so he adjusted his position and let out a long breath.

McKay was snoring within seconds.

As the man began to snore, the woman stepped from the shadows.

She walked silently, stopping alongside McKay.

She caressed his face, feeling guilt over the damage she'd inflicted. Physically and mentally.

McKay was nothing but a vessel for them. A man at the wrong place at the wrong time, forced into these events by his job. Unfortunately for him, the ritual of Abaddon called for the sacrifice of an educated innocent. McKay now fit that bill.

Retrieving her stone box, she opened the lid, removed the sack, and opened the top. She took the mass out, looking at the ancient heart with a chunk of flesh missing.

"Father arise."

The wall rippled and darkened, before Father stepped through.

He was wearing a robe, the front stained red.

McKay rustled and turned, hearing the sounds behind

him. Seeing the woman and Father, he scurried to the head of his bed, legs pulled up tight.

"The fuck? Your burned body was at the scene of that massacre," McKay said, embarrassed with the screech in his voice.

"My earthly body maybe. An immortal never dies."

The woman handed something to Father, McKay unable to see.

The old man stepped towards McKay, staring unnervingly at the detective.

"None of this makes sense. You're responsible for the deaths of your flock. I'll need you to put your hands behind your back," McKay said, feeling emboldened with the familiarity of his job.

"My son. There is nothing left for you here. You've played your role. You've helped us connect the cosmic dots we needed connected. Sleep now."

McKay went to reply, to try and de-escalate the situation, but before he could begin, Father lashed out, his arm moving faster than McKay believed an old man could.

A shriek left his mouth as the nail went through his skin, his skull and lodged into his brain.

A series of grunts followed, his tongue lolled and saliva began to leak profusely.

The last cognizant thought he had was *stop*, as he watched Father and the redhead walk through the black, before it returned to wall.

Bianchi had waited outside McKay's locked office for two hours before he finally got a ride over to his house.

He pounded on the door for some time, before deciding he'd had enough.

He heard a noise from inside, a snort or a huff, and after what he'd seen on that footage, he wasn't about to just leave.

Bianchi kicked the door twice before it gave up and burst inwards.

Entering, he came to an immediate stop when he spotted McKay.

The detective was shuffling around his living room.

His mouth was open, his eyes wide, and he was moaning without interruption. Bianchi could see the drool that coated his chin.

McKay was wearing a t-shirt and shorts and when the man circled around, Bianchi could see that McKay had pissed and shit himself several times over.

At first Bianchi believed that McKay's nose had busted

open again and was bleeding, but when he focused on his face, Bianchi saw that it was because of the nail that protruded from the middle of his forehead.

"Fuck," he said once. He stepped outside and called 911, knowing that his lifelong search of proving Abaddon was a real, physical entity had encountered another roadblock.

When the photo of himself sitting with Brad and the girl had been found in the envelope, he'd held his breath. He didn't believe McKay would've recognized him when he was so young, but he still had been alarmed.

He hit a speed dial number on his phone and waited while it rang.

"Hello." The voice said when they answered.

"McKay's role is complete. I've seen proof. The box has vanished. I'll see you in France."

He hung up. When the sirens approached, he sat and watched the sky darken.

It was times like these Bianchi wished he smoked.

END

I was petrified when I released Ritual.

I absolutely loved the story, and Father is a unique character. It also let me run through some demonology stuff that I've wanted to touch on. But it is a very stark turn from my other releases. Don't get me wrong – if you've read my stuff, you'll know damn well that I like to go dark and awful – but Ritual went to another level. Graphic, sadistic, and in some places gratuitous – all to tell this horrible story. I was surprised at the response. I really was. I want to believe it was because the price point was awesome ($0.99 for the ebook) and the cover is DA BOMB. But, shockingly, people really seemed to connect with the depravity of the story. Beyond surprising was seeing it listed on the recommended reading list for the Stoker's. I never once believed it would carry on further, but what a boost.

Secondly – when I finished Ritual, I barfed out a sequel and a very rough trilogy finale. I've refined the sequel several times now, then waited to see if people would want to read more. It was one particular review that cemented that the demand to see more was there (no, not the 1-star review, which has been a godsend for interest FYI! As of writing this Ritual has six 1-star reviews). It was from my friend Diamond. Her review actually touched on a bit of the direction I'd went with the sequel, and seeing that cosmic connection on Goodreads – all systems were go.

So, as you saw, book two is dedicated to DIE!mond. Thank you for your kind words, but also never sugar coating anything. It's meant a ton!

With Ritual, I did two key bits – Bible Verses and a poem. For this one, I canned the poem part. I felt if I did it again, it would feel like I was reaching to just rehash Ritual. I messaged a few folks and they all said they could live with or without it. Good enough.

As for the Bible Verses. I think they are paramount for two reasons.

The first is that the story within COMMUNION is really based on a rabid, blind faith. Much like the devout can utilize the vagueness of the bible, Father can use his visions and the documents he has to try and open the black heavens. More so though, is McKay and Bianchi's search for answers – no matter the cost.

The bible verses chosen here all relate to Abaddon and Sheol in one form or another. Abaddon and Sheol are co-linked throughout numerous versions of the bible, both as entities/figures as well as places. From the research I've done, neither was ever considered a 'demon' per se, but that's pretty close to the role I've put them in here.

The second reason I chose to use the bible verse structure again is connectivity. While I didn't want to rehash anything directly from Ritual, I did want the trilogy to have a flow and a similar feeling.

Book three will finish the trilogy off, and if you can gather – Bianchi will be in hot pursuit. It will pick up in France and from what I have outlined, I think it's a worthy conclusion to a repulsive character.

I don't want to give anything away here, but if time is on my side, I may be able to get book three out this year (2020) as well. We'll see. I have the bare bones done, but need to flesh it out.

So, thanks so much to all you folks reading this, glad you've come along for the ride.

Most of the time I thank a bunch of folks individually here, but for this one – thank you to everyone out there, you all rock.

Until we meet again.

Steve

ABOUT THE AUTHOR

Steve Stred writes dark, bleak horror fiction.

Steve is the author of three novels, a number of novellas and four collections.

He is proud to work with the Ladies of Horror Fiction to facilitate the Annual LOHF Writers Grant.

Steve is also a voracious reader, reviewing everything he reads and submitting the majority of his reviews to be featured on Kendall Reviews.

Steve Stred is based in Edmonton, AB, Canada and lives with his wife, his son and their dog OJ.

Stevestredauthor.wordpress.com

Twitter @SteveStred
Instagram @SteveStred

Novels

- Invisible

- The Stranger

- Piece of Me

Novellas

- Jane: The 816 Chronicles

- Wagon Buddy

- YURI

- The Girl Who Hid in the Trees

- The One That Knows No Fear

- Ritual

Collections

- Frostbitten: 12 Hymns of Misery

- Left Hand Path: 13 More Tales of Black Magick

- Dim the Sun

- The Night Crawls In

www.ingramcontent.com/pod-product-compliance
Lightning Source LLC
Chambersburg PA
CBHW050956050726

47592CB00007B/2597